The Assemblage

An Open Letter to the Readers

Dear World,

It's as if I've been broken.

That's what I kept telling myself. Maybe my ability to write has been taken. Maybe, just maybe, it was never there, to begin with, and all the "good" writing I've produced was just me patting myself on the back. Maybe I suck. My words will never have an impact. They mean nothing to no one, but me. Yeah… There's probably truth to that but isn't there some truth even in lies. If I saw value there, in the words on a page, someone else would too. Right? Yeah, right.

Your work, no matter what it is, has value!

I truly believe that statement. Believe it with all my heart because it's true. Your work has value, even if that value lies nowhere else than within yourself. Does it bring you joy like writing does me? Bam, instantly you've just proven its value, never undervalue it. Never… That will block you, break you, and darken the world around you.

Darkness brings peace, and peace brings clarity.

That's an opinion. Some people would rather sit in the sun all day, soaking up light, but not me. I'm different. I dislike the day, the beach, the sunlight, the color. I'd rather be in darkness. I'd rather see nothing

than see lies, cheating, hate, and pain. It's disheartening and

everywhere, but it's the truth. And I prefer the truth.

He couldn't cope with the world around him, so he created his own.

I don't know who said this quote first, but I like to think I did. It is the

very quote that pushed me into writing. It's the truth. I didn't and don't

like what I see around me, and so I have created a world to escape

through. That world is being introduced today as you are reading this.

You have a piece of that world in your hands right now. I'm proud of

that.

Welcome to my world!

Before you dive in before this open letter is folded over and you meet

my characters you should know this: I have no idea what this book will

be about at the time of writing this letter. No clue, and so what's on the

pages going forward is as much of a surprise to you as me.

Sincerely, The Author,

Michael Haworth

About M2 and 3

M2 and 3 is the very first story I wrote including the characters Ellie and Ocher, who I would argue now are my most complex characters. At the time I was doing it just to do it. I had these characters in my mind and what better to do with them than write them down somewhere? I don't honestly remember a ton about that time, it was about two years ago now, but I can say it probably went something like this.

I know I was sitting in English class, probably bored out of my mind, (I've always loved, but excelled at English) and bam Ocher popped into my head. A huge man with split personalities and eyes to display which personality had control at what time. At some point, I decided the personalities would end up coming to grips with each other, and that they would sort of become one, but I had no idea why, and that's when the third eye color was born. His eyes would be green when the two sides were at peace, red when the more aggressive side was in control, and orange when his more normal side was in control. It was simple, but missing something, and so I thought of Ellie.

Ellie was simple at first. She was Ocher's way of finding peace between his two sides. She would cause the sides to become one because both sides would love her. Simple, but flat, boring, and cliché. That's what M2 and 3 really was. It was the introduction of these characters and really a proof of concept.

This story is old. It's poorly written, or at least compared to my newer work, and it's flawed. I would argue that it's no more than character notes. A way for me, the author and creator of these characters to flesh them out and get to know them. It was a way for them to become real.

I left this story exactly how I found it. I'm sure there's typos, grammar mistakes, and more, but I didn't want to touch it up. It felt dishonest and wrong to fix it up in the same way it feels wrong to criticize a baby for crying. This story is my start, the first true story where I thought, "Hey this could go somewhere. These characters are alright, and if I work super hard maybe I can give people a world to escape to"

Welcome to the unedited, uncut, messy mind of mine.

Enjoy!

M2 and 3

The room was dark. No movement, no sounds just the faint green glow of two eyes in the corner. A door creaked open revealing a girl. She was short, standing just above five feet, and had pale white skin. Her long black hair rolled down her shoulders. "We will figure out how to beat this, we always find a way.", she said. "You can't give up, because if you give up the whole alliance will follow you… besides, we have never failed before." A man pushed himself up from a desk in the corner of the room. He walked around to the front of the desk and sat on the corner.

"I know we have never failed, but this is different." "We are no match for what is coming." He paused then continued, "We need more than the alliance this time, we need the kid from Amerly."

"What will one new member of the alliance accomplish?" "Why him, why do we need one kid to help us fight this?" She moved closer to the man and flipped the lamp beside him on. "Look at me Ocher." Ocher turned his head, revealing his bright green eyes. "Why does this kid mean so much to you, what don't I know?"

He looked into her eyes and watched the blue ripple like the ocean. He was looking for answers, a way to tell her that they had been wrong this whole time. That he wasn't the first, and she wasn't the second. There was one before them, and many more after them. Ocher needed to tell her the truth, but even he was having trouble wrapping his mind around all the new information he had. He didn't want to worry her, things just started to settle down for the first time in, well in forever. He took a deep breath and started with what he thought she needed to know. "The kid's name is Rex Denton Jr, and he is important to me, but not just because we need his help." Ocher paused and readjusted himself back into her eyes. He continued, "Rex Denton Jr. was the first of the M project to be successful, and that makes him very important for many reasons." A look of disbelief came through into the girl's eyes, and she dropped her chin. "I'm sorry I didn't say anything sooner Ellie, but I wanted to make sure the information I received was valid, and it is valid." Ocher pushed gently under her chin lining their eyes back up. He could see the gears turning in her head. Ocher caressed her cheek and waited

for her response.

"That means you have a brother Ocher, that your father was

Rex Denton Sr." She wasn't mad at him for waiting so long to tell

her. Ellie learned a long time ago that Ocher would tell her anything,

she just had to wait for him to be ready. Everything he did was done

out of pure thought. He had to analyze every situation and find a

way to get ahead of whatever might stand in his way. It was just the

way he was. Ocher turned his head towards the desk and sighed.

She gently turned his head back towards her. Ocher was

trying to keep his eyes from meeting hers. "Ocher look at me, I'm

not mad." "I have no reason to be mad at you." She wrapped her

arms around him resting her head on his chest, "I want to see your

true eyes Ocher, you don't have to hide them with me." Ellie pulled

back a little and looked Ocher in the eyes. They had changed from

the bright green to a fiery orange. "There you go, you have nothing

to hide from me." She paused and looked into Ocher's bright orange eyes. She was looking for the words he needed to hear. "It's okay to be scared or worried you know?"

Ocher caressed her chin, "I'm not scared, or worried." He paused, "I'm just."

Ellie interrupted him. "The word you're looking for is worried." "You are worried the other guy will come out, your scared the red will take over during the battle." "It won't, your visions are not always right, and even if the other guy does come out I'll bring you back." Her eyes started to glow a bright blue color, "I can, and I will always bring you back."

The room became silent, and Ocher turned around. He was looking at a small silver note on his desk. The note was from a woman he had met walking down the street a couple of months ago. It was the source of all the new information, but the contents of the note is not what bothered Ocher. He had always suspected he had a brother, and he already knew his father was an evil genius. Those ideas becoming a reality didn't bother him. No, what bothered him was what the woman said after she handed him the note, "My understanding is this, you know what is coming, read that note, I

think you will find some things that will aid you in winning the

battle you have seen so many times, but… I could be wrong." Then

just like that, she was gone. Leaving Ocher with a weird silver note,

and a lot of questions.

Ellie grabbed Ocher's hand, and he turned back towards her.

"Hey, whatever is on that note, is not in control, you are Ocher." He

stayed silent, he was listening for something. Ellie moved her hand

up to his wrist and laid his hand on her chest. Ocher wanted to feel

and hear her heartbeat. He wanted to feel some peace for a minute.

"Hey, it's okay, use your senses if it helps you think, you know I

don't mind." They both fell into silence. Ocher closed his eyes and

put his other hand against her side. Ocher had heightened senses and

liked to stop and soak in everything at once sometimes. He could

make out letters on paper by touching them and hear heartbeats from

blocks away. It could be overwhelming, but he learned to control it.

Ocher was listening and feeling Ellie's heartbeat because it was

different. It was unreadable by any form of heart rate monitor and could not be heard by anything other than Ocher. He opened his

eyes and pulled his hands away. Ocher liked to hear, feel, and see

anything familiar. He did not like new, anything new took him a

while to adjust too. If it was new he could deal with it, but he

preferred to know everything about anything in his life. He wanted

to know every detail. Smell, taste, touch, sound, and the way things

looked. However, he preferred touch the most. He could feel more

than he could see, and he had excellent vision. "Ocher what's the

plan", Ellie asked?

"step, talk to Rex, find out what he knows, and if he is

willing to help us.", Ocher said with a sort of pleasure. "We will go

from there."

"The great Ocher doesn't have a full plan, I must be

dreaming", Ellie said.

Ocher replied, "Yeah well, Rex is not something that can be

planned for, especially after what he just went through." "I will get

you fully updated in the car, but first we need to pack." Ocher

flipped off the lamp, and they both started walking to their room.

"We are taking a car, don't we have faster ways to get around," Ellie asked? They walked into a little bedroom and pulled two backpacks off a coat hanger. The backpacks were always packed. If something left the bags it went right back when it was finished being used. Whether that item was a weapon, band-aid, candy wrapper, or anything else that might be useful. The bags were different and held different things. Ellie's bag was grey with ocean blue accents and held items that she could use effectively. Ocher's bag was black with orange accents and held items that he found useful. The bags went anywhere that was potentially dangerous, and in Ochers case that was pretty much everywhere.

"Yes, we do have more efficient motives of transportation, but trust me we don't want to rush.", Ocher replied as he stuffed some clothes in an overnight bag. "Besides a road trip will be fun."

"Well I am always down for a road trip, you ready", Ellie asked?

Ocher replied, "Almost." He walked over to a dresser and opened a drawer till it clicked. Ocher moved to the next drawer, then the next, till he had opened eight drawers. Every drawer was open different amounts and had been opened in a specific order. Ocher opened the last drawer all the way. He waited for it to click, and then closed the drawer. Another few clicks came from the drawer, and a door on the side of the dresser popped open. Inside was two pair of sunglasses, a pair of headphones, a folded up bo staff, some gloves, and a necklace. Ocher grabbed everything, but the necklace from the hidden compartment. He handed Ellie a pair of glasses and closed up the dresser. "Now we are ready," Ocher said. He put the gloves, and sunglasses on.

"Alright let's get going we have a long drive ahead of us," Ellie said putting her glasses on. They walked out of a door in the corner of the bedroom and found themselves in a garage.

"It's your turn to pick the vehicle Ellie." Ellie looked around the garage.

"That one", She pointed to an orange car in the corner of the garage. Ocher grabbed a set of keys off of his key rack and threw them towards Ellie. Catching the keys, she said, "Alright I'll drive for the first half." They loaded their bags into the sports car, and the garage door opened revealing the rest of the building. It was a mansion, surrounded by walls. It was the only house for miles. Ellie looked over at Ocher and started the car. He looked back and grabbed her hand.

"Well, I guess it's time to go", He said.

Ellie replied, "Yeah, but we are not done here we will come back." She pulled her glasses off and looked at Ocher. "Ocher, I know that you don't like being out in the world, but we will be fine, you always take good care of me, and I will take care of you." Ocher took his glasses off and looked Ellie in the eyes. He put his hand on her chest and closed his eyes.

"I know that we will be fine, as long as I can hear your heartbeat, and see your eyes.", Ocher said. He opened his eyes, and they changed from orange to bright green.

"You will always be able to hear my heartbeat, and I will never hide my eyes from you." Ellie put her glasses in the cupholder, and Ocher put his on. "Let's get this done so we can come back as soon", She said.

"Agreed", Ocher said. Ellie put the car in drive, and they both said, "To Amerly."

About Into the Mind of Ocher

"Into the Mind of Ocher" is like M2 and 3 in the way that it's old. And I have left it unedited. There isn't really a ton to say about it other than like everything in the world it's not perfect. It's one of my favorite pieces I've ever written, and I hope you enjoy!

Into the Mind of Ocher

Above the clearing, almost so far above it seemed unreal, the moon cast its blue hand-like beam at the ground. The water found disturbance in the form of several falling leaves, and lanterns lining its edge left it slightly brighter than the rock around it. Emilia was sitting, legs crossed, against the shoreline. Her reflection looking up at her, with bright eyes.

She pulled her soaked hair back and studied herself upon the water's surface. It was like looking at her mother, she had the same long dark hair, big eyes, wide smile, and curled backlashes. And sometimes, if she was holding back, she even had similar thoughts as her mother, but those thoughts rare, and usually involved Ocher: her father, who she had, obviously, inherited her mind from.

Emilia rung her towel out, hung it over her shoulder, and stood up. Her reflection followed, and slowly, with a slight glare, her deep green eyes faded to a bright, glowing pink. She loved this pond. No not just the pond, the whole place. The house, the libraries, the pool, her room, her parent's room, the training area, the garage, she loved everything about this home. It was by far her favorite house of the many her parents owned, but, unfortunately, had become the least visited.

Above the clearing, almost so far above it seemed unreal, the moon cast its blue hand-like beam at the ground. The water found disturbance in the form of several falling leaves, and lanterns lining its edge left it slightly brighter than the rock around it. Emilia was sitting, legs crossed, against the shoreline. Her reflection looking up at her, with bright eyes.

She pulled her soaked hair back and studied herself upon the water's surface. It was like looking at her mother, she had the same long dark hair, big eyes, wide smile, and curled backlashes. And sometimes, if she was holding back, she even had similar thoughts as her mother, but those thoughts rare, and usually involved Ocher: her father, who she had, obviously, inherited her mind from.

Emilia rung her towel out, hung it over her shoulder, and stood up. Her reflection followed, and slowly, with a slight glare, her deep green eyes faded to a bright, glowing pink. She loved this pond. No not just the pond, the whole place. The house, the libraries, the pool, her room, her parent's room, the training area, the garage, she loved everything about this home. It was by far her favorite house of the many her parents owned, but, unfortunately, had become the least visited.

Into the Mind of Ocher

Heading straight for the mansion, barely visible through the trees, Emilia kept her head low. Not to hide, but to minimize the cold wind blowing over her face. It had been a nice night of swimming, the first in a while, and now, it had come to an end, and dinner was approaching Emilia's mind faster than a train. Fortunately, her father would be making dinner right about now, and they could all sit down to rest for a moment. An act that had become rare lately, as the date of the battle drew closer, sucking more and more life from the air with every passing day.

Emilia hated this feeling, but in her short life, had come to deal with it. She had to, it had been a burden on her shoulders since day one. Her eyes darkened, shifting to blood red.

The man in black, he was the reason for such an odd life. He was the reason Emilia would never meet her aunt, he was the reason her uncle was so broken, the man in black was the reason life was so difficult.

The entrance to the mansion became clearly visible as Emilia came through the trees. Almost every window was dark and closed off with curtains. It was time to go inside, as soon as the lights were shut off from the outside, Emilia was to be home, or at least heading that way.

As soon as she stepped in front of the huge front doors, they swung open, and beyond them, light escaped from the gaps between the newly formed opening and her father. Emilia's eyelids snapped over the red, and when they reopened, the deep green had returned.

"I heard you coming, dinner is ready, your mother has already made you a plate. Feeling alright?", Ocher's deep, passionate voice boomed, as his emerald eyes skimmed around Emilia.

He knew she wasn't alright, he always knew, there was no point in lying.

"Today we shall fall, so tomorrow…"

"We can rise", Ocher finished the moto for Emilia. "Wise girl… it's almost like your mine", He joked.

Emilia couldn't help but smile out of the corner of her mouth, it was rare for her father to pop a joke. There wasn't a day in her life that she didn't remember her father saying these words. They had just stuck with her since… well forever.

"Perhaps it's time I show you something... Something in my mind.

Let's eat first though... come in, it's getting chilly", Ocher said resting his large hand on Emilia's shoulder, and guiding her inside. He shut the door behind them, turning straight for the kitchen, gently pushing Emilia the whole way.

"Is mom worried", She asked, as they walked past a couple of familiar doors.

"Your moms not all that worried, not about what you think... No, your mom is more worried about you than anything else", Ocher answered, his voice low so it wouldn't carry down the flat hall.

"Are you worried?"

"Always. Although I must admit that recently things have really settled down. No word has come from the Master Mansion in a while... well, none that is alarming." Ocher clamped his hand tighter to her shoulder, and hung a left, into a small entranceway, a little way from the kitchen. "Listen your mother is very worried about you, and I'd be lying if I said I wasn't. However, worrying is not productive, and now more than ever we need to charge forward with our countermeasures. Just keep your head up, eyes open, and whatever you do, don't become unfocused… This will all be over very soon, I promise. And as I said I need to show you something after dinner.", He said in a whisper.

Ocher's voice calmed Emilia, and she felt as though six tons had just lifted from her shoulders. He let go of her, they walked into the kitchen, greeted Ellie, and sat down.

Ellie sat with them, her plate full of pizza, and sparked a conversation, with a smile on her face. It was then that Emilia realized something, her mother, she was beautiful. It wasn't the first time she had ever thought this, but it sure had never hit her this hard. How was her mother, after such a rough couple weeks… Not even just weeks, but years, putting a smile on her face? Emilia couldn't even manage a smile after a bad day of training. She couldn't imagine being able to do it after so many hardships, and deaths.

Emilia would never amount to even half of what her parents did, she was sure of it.

"So how was the pond honey?", Ellie asked, her eyes their usual mesmerizing selves, as she took a bite of pizza.

"Cold… Peaceful though, very peaceful", Emilia said, her voice scratching up her throat.

Ellie widened her smile and dropped the pizza on her plate. She did this often and was about to start barraging Emilia with questions.

"You okay Emilia?", She asked?

"Yes."

"Nothing at all you want to talk about, no worries you may have, nothing at all", She added.

"No", Emilia said taking a bite of her own pizza. Ocher looked at her, his eyes swirling with different greens.

…don't become unfocused…

Emilia let Ellie barrage her with questions, answering them all with a simple yes or no. Of course, even if she wasn't worried, this is how she would have answered the questions anyway, and so her mother didn't really question the short words.

As dinner zoomed by, the conversation had changed many times. Starting with the barrage of questions, leading into what would be served for breakfast, and finally landing on the thing that had been bothering Emilia so much: her uncle. He had fallen into a depressed state once again, something that wasn't abnormal. It was odd, however, that he had seemed to disappear from existence two weeks before.

"His alter ego hasn't been seen for almost two and a half weeks Ocher. Don't you think that's a bit unlike Rex?", Ellie said, trying to drill into Ocher's mind. "Emilia, stay out of my head", She snapped.

Emilia pulled herself away from her mother's mind, just enough to make Ellie think she was fully removed. Ocher wasn't kidding, Ellie was worried, and her mind was running at full speed. There was no way to understand what was going on from the distance Emilia was at, and she pulled completely from her mother's mind, injecting herself back into the conversation.

"He's been depressed before mom, maybe he's just taking time", Emilia said not really believing the words coming from her mouth.

"I agree, my brother has disappeared before. It's not uncommon, he'll show up, perhaps he is just preparing for the return of the man in black. I wouldn't put it past him. He's clever sometimes and almost always ahead", Ocher said slurping the rest of his shakedown and turning his head to his wife.

"So, neither of you are worried?"

"We didn't say that", Ocher and Emilia said simultaneously.

"I'm very worried", Ocher added. "However, I feel putting all of our resources into finding my brother is not a good use of energy. We need to prepare for the worst, and my brother, unfortunately, I may add, does not fit into that equation."

Emilia rose from her chair and rested herself upon the table with her arms. Frustration was flowing through her veins.

"I think he simply is resting. We all saw his last fight, it was brutal, he's probably laying low to heal up, adjust himself... He was struggling with some things last time I saw him. Maybe he's just taking some time to cope... or more time to cope", Emilia said, her hands curling up on the table top, as her eyes drifted to a dark purple.

"Perhaps… my brother is known for taking his time", Ocher said plainly.

Dinner wrapped up in silence, Ellie cleaned up, walked down the hall, turned to her bedroom, and disappeared. Ocher sat down next to Emilia at the table, whose eyes had landed back on the green.

"Are you and mom going to be okay", She asked keeping her voice low.

"Yes. Always", Ocher said his voice low too. "Give me your hands."

He put his hands out, Emilia raised her own, set them down on his, and he led them to his forehead.

"You're sure you want me to enter your mind again… even after last…"

"You need to see this", Ocher interrupted, placing her thumbs on opposite sides of his temple. He closed his eyes and nodded to show he was ready.

Emilia mimicked her father and closed her eyes. She loosened her shoulders. Her eyes rolled over under their lids, settled straight again, and snapped open. A purple haze flowed from them, projecting a sense of power over the kitchen counter, into the atmosphere, and throughout the house.

The scene around Emilia rolled out of sight, she fell through a purple smoke and landed, feet first, next to Ocher. In front of them, a familiar stretch of land, in fact, Emilia had just left it; the pond was much brighter under the sun.

"Where are we", Emilia said, her voice dreamy.

"You know the answer to that Emilia. Explore, see if you can find why I brought you to this memory specifically. It shouldn't be too hard to find."

Emilia nodded, walking across the silver rock below her, she glanced back and saw Ocher was watching her, or rather barely following her with his gaze.

She walked three laps around the glimmering water before stopping in front of her father and again asking why they were here, in this what seemed to be empty memory. He shook his head, and said,

"You haven't explored enough… Perhaps, what you're looking for is not beached, but rather submerged.

"Tell you what I'm going to speed this up a bit. What is naturally round, but never a perfect sphere?"

"A pearl", Emilia said immediately.

"Correct… So, what do you think my thoughts were when I found this in the pond when your mother and I were taking a midnight stroll", Ocher said dipping his hand into the water beside him and pulling a large white sphere out.

Emilia studied the pearl as it dropped into her hand. It was perfect, her father was right, this stone looked like a pearl, but it was simply to spherical, and light.

"I assume you studied it, figured out what it was made of, where it may have come from", She said rolling the fake pearl around in her palm with her thumb.

"It's M-X. The material your uncle's suit is made of, the material the man in blacks suit is made of. He had found our hideout", Ocher said putting his hands out. Emilia dropped the pearl in them.

"Wait so the man… He knows where we are, he knows about this place… we are staying here dad. We are in trouble", Emilia said thinking her father was crazy.

Ocher said nothing, he obviously expected the reaction he got. He brought his arm back, and threw the pearl, dead center, into the pond. The spot around the pearl rippled as it hit the surface of the water, and as it sank, the water stuttered and bubbled. A deep reddish glow exploded out from the point, filling the water first, then slowly it came up to the shoreline.

"No Emilia… He hadn't found us… We found him", He said, and all of the sudden, in less than a second, Emilia understood, the man in black had made a mistake.

And not just any mistake, one that gave her father information. A mistake that had sealed the man in blacks fate, they were now the ones a step ahead.

Emilia's Gift

Tick...Tick...Tick...

The clock irked Ocher. He covered his ears, closing his eyes attempting to drown the noise, but still, it came through his hands.

Tick...Tick...Tick....

"Escape, run, get away." The voice raced through Ocher's mind. It was unhappy.

"We can't leave", Ocher said.

The voice raspy and desperate made an angry sound, somewhere between a grunt and a scream. It wanted mayhem, needed it to survive, but Ellie needed Ocher now more than ever. He pushed the voice away.

"We'll be back before she awakes."

Ocher shook the voice again.

"She won't even know."

"Shut up. We're staying right here. She needs us, and if I remember correctly you love her too." Ocher said with a growl.

"Come on it bothers you too."

"Not nearly as much as you do."

Ocher got up from the bench, steadying himself, and cracking his neck. He released, ever so slowly, his ears from his grasp, letting a big breath out. Breathe in slowly, he thought, then out.

Tick...Tick...Tick…

"We're improving."

"We? I'm doing all the work. I've learned how to focus my hearing. I did. We're doing *nothing*. I am." His voice was muffled in his head. It seemed the voice decided to drown him out.

"If I'm doing nothing, then so are you."

Ocher didn't answer. He had nothing to say. Primary control was his after all, why would he answer to this thing in his head? He controlled it, not it him.

He pushed the huge wooden door open, making sure to minimize noise. There it was, the clock, right there across the room, noisy as ever. He swept the room with his intense orange gaze, then stopped at the bed across from the clock. His beautiful wife was sleeping, each breath taken by her causing a nasty crack.

Broken ribs, Ocher thought. He focused harder.

Thump.Thump.Thump.Thump…

Her heart was faster than normal. She hurt. She was in pain and it was on him. Why couldn't he say no? He knew the consequences of having a baby… The risks involved with his seed. Numbers don't lie, and he ran them a thousand times, yet she convinced him like she always did.

"I love you", Ocher said, kissing her on the cheek and pulling a blanket over her. "You'll heal quick enough, you always do."

Ellie's dazzling blue eyes rolled open. "I know Ocher. I love you too, but please don't worry about me. My abilities will take care of me, they just…"

"…need to rejuvenate. I understand sweetheart. Get some rest."

Ellie's eyes fell back behind their lids. "Ocher?", She said.

"Yes sweetheart?"

"It's not her fault."

"What?"

"Emilia, our daughter. It's not her fault. Take care of her while I'm healing."

Ocher nodded, agreeing with Ellie. "But you need care." He rubbed his finger across her hairline.

"Yeah, but so does she. Just promise me you'll at least hold her."

"What if…"

Ellie slowly shook her head and opened her eyes. "You won't big guy. You'll be gentle with her just like your gentle with me." She smiled. "Promise you'll hold her?'

"I promise." Ocher ran his finger once more across her forehead, and she closed her eyes. He kissed her. "Get some rest beauty."

He watched her for a minute, taking in ever flinch, crunch, and breath. She was restless. She hurt.

"She's beautiful", The voice said, it's voice less raspy.

"Yeah, she is. Inside and out."

"Ellie's beautiful, but I was speaking of the child."

Ocher turned to look at the crib. Emilia was sitting up, just staring at him through her… Her eyes had changed colors. They were green and now… Pink. She giggled and back to green they changed.

"She's got emotional based…", Ocher started

"...eyes."

"Like mine."

Ocher stunned, stared for a moment. Emilia hiccupped, and her eyes turned red for a brief time, then back to green.

She's gifted, Ocher thought. She's like us. His heart warmed up and grew as the infant giggled and smiled like her mother. He kneeled.

"Aren't you the adorable."

She hiccupped again, then seeing her father's hand laughed. Ocher reached out, waiting for her to move, then apparently deciding his hand was something safe to touch, she reached back.

Their hands connected.

Ocher's head spun. For a second, he swore he had fallen asleep, then all of his senses spiked, and he thought he'd been punched. He fell to his side, and Emilia started to wail. Tears streamed from her eyes; they shifted to gray. She threw Ocher's hand away.

"Whoa... Shhhh...", Ocher said. "Shhhh. It's okay, just quiet down so your mother can rest."

But the baby didn't care if her mother rested or not, and she screamed louder. Ocher covered his ears.

"Please be quiet."

"Hold her", The raspy voice returned.

"What?"

The voice sighed. "Hold the infant. You promised Ellie and quite frankly I don't see another way to calm her, do you?"

Ocher thought for a second before concluding the voice (perhaps for the first time ever) was right. He reached for his baby. "Come here. Don't you want to be held?' Emilia let out piercing scream, rolling away. "Come on please."

Before Ocher knew what, he was doing he had picked Emilia up, and just like that she was content.

"I'm proud of you big guy."

Ocher turned. Ellie was up, sitting against the backboard, watching her daughter giggle.

"She has your eyes Ocher."

Ocher shook his head. "I strongly disagree. My eyes are terrifying and cruel. Hers are soft and beautiful. She's got your eyes", He said.

"Eh… I don't think so." Ellie got up and started rubbing Emilia's back. "You try. Here." She helped Ocher's hand to the infants back and showed him how to slowly work in circles.

"She's happy." Emilia's head fell on Ocher's shoulder.

Ellie's smile extended even further. "Of course, she is Ocher, your rubbing her, and rocking her. She feels loved and safe. Anyone is happy when they feel that way."

"Do you feel that way?"

"Safe and loved?"

"Yeah. Do you feel like that here… You know here with me?", Ocher said rocking on his heels.

"Yes, I do. I feel safe and loved all the time, which is quite the feat Ocher, considering our lifestyle."

Ocher remained silent for a moment. "Would you tell me if you didn't feel safe?"

"Ocher if I didn't feel safe do you honestly think I would have agreed to have a baby with you?'

"Well no, but…"

"You dork. I love you!" Ellie laughed. "Here try patting her." She pulled Ocher's hand out, pressing it back quickly. "There you go just like that."

Ocher kept patting Emilia, listening to her gurgle, and giggle. Ellie just watched and sat back down. Her breathing was still rough. Ocher could tell she was sore, but she seemed happy. She had a huge smile on her face and her eyes were as stunning as ever.

Then it happened. Emilia's tiny hand raised, her thumb and index finger uncurled, and she placed her palm on Ocher's forehead. Both their pupils dilated, and their irises greened. Emilia sniffled, and the world seemed to unroll around Ocher.

He was falling. Lights of every color flashed around him, and despite the feeling of traveling down fast, the tunnel of light was windless.

Ocher landed feet first into a solid stance, his vision blurry. He blinked into focus. Stunned. The woman in front of him was beautiful. Her eyes were a beautiful mix of blue and green, and her dark hair rolled down her shoulders. She laughed, putting a handout.

"Hey dad", She said. "I don't understand it either. I just know who you are."

"Emilia?"

"Yes, it's me. Do you know where we are?"

Ocher couldn't care less where they were. He was more worried about when they were or how.

"How old are you?'

Emilia seemed confused by the question. "I guess I'm still only a week old. I don't think we time traveled. The lack of sensory makes me believe we are…"

"Inside a mind."

"Yeah, how did you know?"

Ocher looked at his daughter closer, she was just like her mother, stunning. "I've had my fair share of mental experiences. You must be telepathic." He could hardly believe his statement. The closest

thing to a telepath he'd ever met was Freya and she was only empathic.

"Yeah, I guess that makes sense", Emilia said looking around.

"What?"

"Well, it makes sense that I'm telepathic. Mom's telekinetic

right? And with a mind like yours…"

"…they came together. The powers to make one, telepathy. It

does add up. I should've guessed."

Emilia nodded. "Yeah. So where are we exactly? This is your

mind after all."

Ocher focused around them and took the scene in. They were

high up on a building overlooking the ocean. A big gust of wind blew a

cloud of dust up from the concrete roof. The muddled scene cleared.

The skyline filled with stars, the city below with the noise of bustling

traffic, and the air with the smell of salt. He knew exactly where they

were. He remembered this night well.

He looked over. Ellie was laying on a towel looking up at the stars, Ocher's hand firmly holding hers. She was humming, nodding her beautiful head to the sound, and Ocher was simply listening.

"You're too cute when you sleep", Ellie said, breaking her hum.

Ocher's orange eyes opened, and he grunted. "I'm not sleeping. I'm listening."

"Oh yeah?"

"Yeah. Sometimes listening can help us remember. I think we forget to just take in scenes sometimes. That people treat life like a movie and rush to the action."

Elie's eyes deepened and started to glow an intense blue. She rolled onto Ocher's chest, placing her ear to his sternum.

"And what do you hear big guy?", She said.

Ocher focused. "Hmm… Below there's an angry child. He's hungry, but they don't have any food or money. His mother is using the last of it to make him a sandwich, starving herself for him, but she's still hopeful."

"How do you know?"

"Because she's telling the boy a story. Our story. She's telling him that we will bring peace to people like them."

A tear slid from Ellie's eye and fell on Ocher's chest. Both felt the warmth and smiled.

"You brought us here on purpose?"

"Yeah. The boy's like us Ellie. He has abilities. He's been cast out by society because of his difficulty with controlling them. It's unfortunate. People believe we are born with these abilities like a heart and that they just beat for you, but they don't. We must learn."

Ellie ran her hand up Ocher's chest, snuggling closer to him. "You want to recruit him?"

Ocher nodded, caressing his beautiful wife. "I want to do much more than that. I'm going to offer them a place to stay. It's unfair they must live here. The mom lost her job, the child's right to education, and now they struggle every day. We're going to fix that."

"You're a good man Ocher." She closed her eyes. "Can we just lay here a bit longer. We don't get a lot of time alone these days."

"Of course,", Ocher said.

"Tell me what else you hear."

Ocher focused once more, wrapping an arm around Ellie. "A baby was just born in the hospital a couple of blocks over. She's six pounds and two ounces. Hmmm... A little boy lost his first tooth tonight. His dad is slipping the tooth fairy money under his pillow now. Your heart is steady, beautiful, and strong."

"Ocher?"

"Yeah?"

"I want a baby of my own."

Ocher's eyes bolted open. He tightened his hold around Ellie. "We can go to the hospital and..."

"No silly with you. I want a baby with you." Ellie sat up. He could tell she knew what he was thinking.

"We don't know that. I heal fast and you would be careful, and you would be a great father. I just... I think we should think about it." Ellie looked at Ocher hopefully. "You will think about it won't you big guy? Please?"

Ocher could tell this meant a lot to her. He'd seen her excited about many things, but never like she was around children, and he knew her own would make her happy. He had no choice. He'd need to think about it.

"I'll think about. I promise, but for now, we have a child below that needs us."

"Oh, thank you so much!" Ellie pecked Ocher on the cheek, and the scene blurred.

Emilia stepped beside her father, who'd been on his knees watching. He took a deep breath and stood.

"You didn't want a child?"

Ocher shook his head. "It wasn't that I didn't want one. I was just scared. We didn't know what a child from us would do, or how the pregnancy would work." He turned to face Emilia. "I just didn't want to lose your mother."

"But she's okay."

"Yeah. I'm grateful for that. Her chances of surviving were getting very slim, quickly."

Emilia's smile faded. "I hurt her?"

"No. I did."

"I doubt she has the same opinion."

"I know she doesn't, but it's the truth. I hurt her. I knew the consequences", Ocher dropped his head.

"She's beautiful."

"She is. Inside and out. She's much more than I deserve. She's so kind, and innocent. She's never done anything that can't be forgiven, but I have."

Emilia's smile returned. "You can't believe that."

"Why?"

"Because you trust her. You love her, I can see that, feel it, and if she thinks you're worthy of her love then you are."

The scene exploded in a burst of light. Ocher was standing, baby Emilia in one arm, and Ellie looking worried holding the other.

"Ocher what happened?", She said.

"Our daughter", He said, "She's telepathic."

The End for Now

So, you made it to the end. Thank you for taking the time to read this. For diving into the messy uprising of a world and looking into a tiny sliver of it. I plan on bringing a more formal book out by the end of the year. That's the goal. That's my deadline, but I bet you I don't make it. It'll probably take a smidge longer to iron out the wrinkles, but until then you have this and whatever I decide to release and show. Till then even I'm in the dark about what's coming.

The last work in this book is "Emilia's Gift" That's my newest work. I dare say some of my best. It was a last-minute thing. This book was supposed to be strictly old work. Work that I'd finished already, and I deemed important to my growth as a writer, but I had to include it. I couldn't leave it unseen. Does it have any true looks into the future of my characters? I don't know. I haven't planned that far, but I had the idea and so to get back into a flow, I wrote it.

Thank you! See you all very soon.

The Author,

Michael Haworth

Me the Author

There isn't much to say here. Um… I enjoy reading, writing, and video games. Beyond that, I don't really enjoy much of anything. I love animals. I was born in April 2000, and if I could be anything it would be a successful author. I'm just me.

Made in the USA
Middletown, DE
21 April 2022

64575878R00036